The Greedy, Mischievious TURTOISE and the Inquisitive LION

Mariagorretti E.O. Okoro

To order additional copies of this book, contact:
Xlibris
844-714-8691
www.Xlibris.com
Orders@Xlibris.com

ISBN:	Softcover	978-1-6698-0383-6
	EBook	978-1-6698-0382-9

Print information available on the last page

Rev. date: 08/25/2022

The Greedy, Mischievious TURTOISE and the Inquisitive LION

Mariagorretti E.O. Okoro

Once upon a time, there was a greedy and mischievous tortoise who had no shell. One day, the tortoise was so hungry and went on a journey to search for some palm kernels, which was the tortoise favorite food.

As tortoise was going, he put on his knapsack: Tortoise was going, Ajambenay, was going, Ajambenay (the great tortoise), Going!, Going!, Going!, Going!, Going!, Going!

The tortoise meets the 1St palm tree; tortoise asked the palm tree "How many palm kernels have you ripened". The palm kernel tree said "Ten".

Tortoise was going, Ajambenay, was going, Ajambenay, Going!, Going!, Going!,
Going!, Going!, Going!

Then the tortoise kept on going and met the 2nd palm tree. The tortoise asked the palm kernel tree, "How many palm kernels have you ripened". The palm tree replied "30". So the tortoise went on its way searching for more ripened palm kernels.

As the tortoise was going, he was not impressed because the whole palm kernels was not ripened as he thought. Because the tortoise was so greedy, he did not want just 10 or 30 palm kernels, so he kept on going from tree to tree.

Therefore, he continued to ask each one of the palm trees, "How many palm kernels have ripened."

Finally, the tortoise met a palm tree, whose palm kernels were all ripened and just right for the tortoise to pick. As he was plucking the palm kernels from the tree, he put some of them in his knapsack and was eating some of them.

He was trying to make sure that all of the palm kernels were picked from the palm tree.

Suddenly, one of the palm kernels fell into the river. Instead of him to forget about the palm kernel that had fallen into the water, because of his greediness,

he left the rest of the palm kernels that he had picked and then jumped into the river and started searching for the palm kernel that fell into the river.

He then met a fish in the river and he asked the fish "Pardon me, fish have you seen a palm kernel". The fish said "No!" So the tortoise caught that fish and put it in his knapsack. The tortoise then saw another fish and asked it whether it had seen a palm kernel. The fish replied, "No!"

So the tortoise also caught that fish and put it in his knapsack too. He continued to swim and ask other fishes whether they had seen his palm kernel.

After asking every fish that he met the same question epeatedly, each fish would reply no, the tortoise would then catch each fish and put it in his knapsack. So he prepared to go home because his knapsack was filled up with so many fishes.

The tortoise then swam out of the river and started walking home. With so much enthusiasm and excitement, the tortoise said "What a joy of catching so many fishes and picking so many palm kernels."

As he was on his way home, he met all types of animals. The first animal was an elephant. As the elephant walked towards the tortoise, his movement shook the ground, which caused the tortoise to fall down. Immediately, the tortoise got back up with his knapsack firmly tight on his back.

The elephant asked the tortoise "Do you need some help because the load on your back looks very heavy." The tortoise shook his head and said "No!" in a trembling tone. The tortoise told the elephant that he was on his way to give his daughter some medicine.

He then explained that his daughter was very stubborn and that he had told her not to marry on the other side of the village near the river. But she refused and went there to get married. Unfortunately, she fell terribly ill.

After the tortoise heard that his daughter was ill, he was also so stubborn enough, that he cared so much for her and went to retrieve the medicine that was necessary to make her get well. The elephant understood and left the tortoise to continue his itinerary.

But the tortoise had no sick daughter or medicine in his knapsack; it was just a trick to confuse and deceive the elephant.

He kept on going and suddenly he met a giraffe and the giraffe asked the tortoise "Do you need any help with that load on your back" but the tortoise would reply "No!" The tortoise would then explain to the giraffe the same thing that he had told the elephant.

The tortoise told the giraffe that he was on his way to give his daughter some medicine. He then explained again that his daughter was very stubborn and that he had told her not to marry on the other side of the village near the river. But she refused and went there to get married. Unfortunately, she fell terribly ill.

After the tortoise heard that his daughter was ill, he was also so stubborn enough, that he cared so much for her and went to retrieve the medicine that was necessary to make her get well. And said that he must go quickly before she becomes more sicker than she is.

The giraffe then told the tortoise to have a safe trip and to send his best wishes to his daughter allowing the tortoise to continue his journey.

But the tortoise had no sick daughter or medicine in his knapsack; everything that he told to the giraffe was all a lie and made up to mislead the giraffe.

As the tortoise kept on going, he met a goat, hyena and a zebra. They all asked the tortoise if he needed help because the load on his back looked very heavy. But the tortoise would continue to tell each one of the animals no.

He would also explain to them the same thing that he told the elephant and the giraffe.

He was then confronted by a lion who asked him if he needed some help with his heavy knapsack. The tortoise told him no and gave an explanation why. After talking to the lion the tortoise thought that he had nothing to do with any of the animals.

He thought that he was free at last. But he did not realize that something strange was going to happen to him. He never thought that the lion would come back. So the tortoise felt relaxed like a newborn baby.

As he reached home he dropped his knapsack that was filled with palm kernels and fishes on the floor. He then went to get his ingredients ready so that he could cook his fish. He then pulled out a fish from his knapsack and put it in the pot and placed it on the fire.

As he was cooking the fish, he waited for it to get done. When he finished cooking, he began to eat the fish.

While he was eating the fish there was a knock on the door. And guess who it was? So the tortoise got up and walked to the door to check who was knocking. Surprisingly it was the lion. The tortoise could not believe it.

He was so shocked that when he saw the lion, he started shivering. The lion started pounding on the door so hard and broke the door down with his mighty strength.

The tortoise never expected that the lion would ever comeback to see that the tortoise was lying since the tortoise had no medicine but that there was only fishes and palm kernel in his knapsack all along. Furthermore, the lion asked the tortoise why he lied.

The tortoise said that he has already given his daughter the medicine. The lion said "Hmm Hmm!" The lion then walked over to where the fishes were and took over the whole fishes.

At the same time, he took the tortoise and grabbed the wooden mortar that the tortoise had used to pound food with. The lion then covered the tortoise with it. The lion went back to eat the fish, while the tortoise lay captive in the mortar crying for help.

The lion did not listen and ignored the tortoise's cries and resumed eating his fish. As the lion finished eating the fish, he then gathered the bones and threw them under the wooden mortar where the tortoise was, so that the tortoise could eat the bones.

He kept on putting the bones under the mortar after every fish he had eaten.

When the lion had finished all of the fishes, the lion left and forgot to uncover the tortoise, leaving the tortoise trapped under the wooden mortar. The tortoise was trapped in the mortar for days.

One day the lion remembered that he did not release the tortoise from the wooden mortar. The lion then went back again to the tortoise home to free the tortoise. As the lion tried to release the tortoise from the mortar, it was so difficult for the mortar to come off the tortoise. It was stuck on the tortoise.

The lion kept on trying to release the tortoise but he was unable to free the tortoise. So the lion went to go get a saw to cut an opening on both sides of the mortar, so that the tortoise feet could come out and to cut an opening in the middle for the tortoise's head to stick out too.

So the tortoise's head, legs and arms came out through the openings that the lion had made. The imprints on the tortoise's shell were due to the lion trying to free the tortoise, while hitting and banging on the wooden mortar.

And this is how the tortoise got his shell, all because of his greed and mischief.